O9-BHK-059

That's Not How You Play Soccer, Daddy!

Written by Sherry Shahan

Illustrated by Tatjana Mai-Wyss

Ω
PEACHTREE
ATLANTA

For my grandsons Michael Patrick O'Connor and Cooper Alan Wommack—
Let the games begin! Love, Granola

—S. S.

Thanks to Joe, Pam, Kati, and the rest of the team

—T. M.-W.

Ω

Published by
PEACHTREE PUBLISHERS
1700 Chattahoochee Avenue
Atlanta, Georgia 30318-2112
www.peachtree-online.com

Text © 2007 by Sherry Shahan
Illustrations © 2007 by Tatjana Mai-Wyss

Art direction by Loraine M. Joyner
Composition by Melanie McMahon Ives

Illustrations created in watercolors, colored paper, and collage on printmaking paper.

Printed in Singapore
10 9 8 7 6 5 4 3 2 1
First Edition

Library of Congress Cataloging-in-Publication Data
Shahan, Sherry.
  That's not how you play soccer, Daddy / written by Sherry Shahan ; illustrated by
Tatjana Mai-Wyss. -- 1st ed.
      p. cm.
  Summary: An unusual game with his father in the park shows team captain Mikey that
soccer can be a fun game to play.
  ISBN 13: 978-1-56145-416-7
  ISBN 10: 1-56145-416-8
 [1. Soccer--Fiction. 2. Fathers and sons--Fiction.] I. Mai-Wyss, Tatjana, 1972- ill. II.
Title. III. Title: That is not how you play soccer, Daddy.

PZ7.S52784Tha 2009
[E]--dc22
                                           2007006878

"Grab a ball!" Coach calls.
"It's time to play soccer!"

Mikey is team captain.
His shiny new uniform says
Hot Diggity Diner.

"I'll be the best captain ever!" he boasts.

Coach splits the team
in two:

Shirts-In
Shirts-Out.

"Now dig in and win!"
she says.

It's stop and slow for Shirts-In. Mikey yells,

"Go!
Go!
Go!"

Uh-oh. It's a heave-ho throw.
Coach calls, "No-o-o hands!"

Moms and dads shout,
"Boot it!"
"Kick it!"
"Lickety-split it!"

But Mikey's daddy shouts,
"EEE-gads!"

"Arf, arf!" barks Mikey's dog.

"Down, Socks! Down!"
Poor Daddy.
Socks drags him off for a walk.

"Have fun, son!"

Mikey doesn't look back.
He cuts and runs,
        rat-a-tat-tack-ing the ball.
It blasts to the goal posts.
Mikey digs in.

The goalie blocks, arms crossed.

It's a sideways slam! Heads bonk. BAM!

b a m

"Ouch!" Mikey shouts.

Coach sets up red cones.

"Cut in!" she calls.
"Cut out!"

But Shirts-In spot an anthill.

Shirts-Out spin into whirlybirds.

"Hey, guys, that's out-of-bounds!" Mikey shouts.

va room

VA-ROOM!
Mikey leads his team back in.
"Don't let anyone steal,"
     Coach says.
          "Drill!
               Drill!
                    Drill!"
Mikey huffs and puffs,
     too pooped to punt.

"Good job," Coach says at last.
She blows her whistle. "Remember,
we have a big game next week.
Practice!
Practice!
Practice!"

Shirts-In run up and
Shirts-Out run down,
    slapping high fives.
Mikey toes it to the sideline.

He waves to his friends.
"Smell you later, alligators."

"When your tail's a little
straighter," they yell back.

Daddy is waiting. So is Socks. Mikey jumps in Daddy's pick-up truck.

They zoom across town to the park.

"Hey, it's lunchtime," Daddy says. "How about a snack?"

"Can we practice first?" Mikey asks. "For our big game?
We have to win,

win,

WIN!"

"Sure," Daddy says. "Let's have fun!"

Socks noses the ball.
"No way," Mikey says.
"Dogs can't play soccer!"

"Daddy, do you know all the rules?" Mikey asks.

Daddy smiles. "You bet I do!"

Mikey calls the coin toss. "Tails. I lost. You get the first shot."

Daddy kicks.
     Oops, a miss!

Daddy stumbles,
     tumbles,
          tangles,
               falls.

He grabs the ball.

"No hands allowed!" Mikey shouts.

Too late.

FOUL!

"Daddy, that's not how
        to play!"

Daddy gives a left kick,
a right kick,
a shoelace-untied kick.
Whoops!
A lose-a-shoe kick.

Daddy grins. "Think I'll
lose the other shoe too!"

Shoes fly high.
        Up,
                Up,
                        Up!

The ball flies across
the line.
        Zig,
                Zag…

ZOOM!

Mikey boots the ball back in.

Daddy gives it a heel-toe spin.

"Go for the poles!" Mikey shouts. "That's our goal!"

Daddy trips, head over heels.

Mikey frowns. "Stop goofing off."

Daddy laughs. "The grass tickles my feet."

"Then put on your cleats." Mikey says.

Daddy pulls Mikey into a hug.
"Just have fun, son."

There's a belly tickle,
a belly chuckle.
Mikey wiggles,
then he tickles too.

"Penalty!" Daddy scolds. "No hands allowed!"

Too late.

It's a tummy-tickle foul!

"You win, Daddy," Mikey says.
"Can we practice again tomorrow?"

"If we take off our shoes," Daddy says.
"And forget the rules."
Mikey kicks off his shoes.
"Come on, Socks. You can play too!"

t i p t o

Skip-hop,
Flip-drop,
a tip-top romp.

Whoop-eee-whee!

Soccer is fun!